Love Don't Love

Ty Eros

This fictional work is purely from the heart, mind, and soul of the author and any similarities to actual persons or situations are completely coincidental.

ISBN: 0692551913
ISBN-13: 978-0692551912

DEDICATION

This book is dedicated to everyone that's ever had a dream. No matter how big or small or crazy it may seem go for it! You may be afraid of failing or even think that you're too old, but it's never too late and you'll never know your full potential unless you try. I never thought I'd really publish a book but here it is today. I want to take a moment and encourage every person reading these words right now to believe in yourself and never let anyone still your hope, your faith, or your dreams.

CONTENTS

CONTENTS

Acknowledgments

ACKNOWLEDGMENTS

It's been a long time coming and I want to thank everyone who encouraged, supported and pushed me to write this book. I won't mention too many names because I don't want to forget and offend anyone. However, I definitely have to give a shout out to my *"author brother"* Mokha Kentwood and my H-town homie, Rashad Howard. These two men really stood behind me and pushed my lazy butt, without these guys this book would still be a half written story on my laptop and I want them to know just how much I appreciate them. Lastly I want to thank **YOU**, yes you the person reading this book right now. No matter how much work went into it if you hadn't brought it all of that would be for nothing. So again I say thank you and I hope that this book does you well in every way possible.

"Love Don't Love"

I used to be in love till I learned
Love don't love
It has no heart or concern
It gives a bittersweet kiss of misery
and drives a rod of deceit right
through your core
I've learned to live within the
shelter of my own mind
Flaws and all I've accepted myself
Gained the strength to see all the
beauty within the ashes
I feel the warmth of solitude's
embrace
Standing in silence and living
alone
I face the big reality
Love don't love

Dr. Paul J. Kingston, III

Chapter 1

It's A Surprise

I pinned the words of that poem shortly after I had discovered the harsh reality of the game called love in my own life. I entitled it the same as the story I'm about to tell you. The story of my true life lesson on how love can take all your joy, fuck your friends, tear your heart to shreds, and ultimately make a fool out of you. I'm not bitter or opposed to ever being in another relationship, but I'm definitely going to be cautious about it if I do. I've officially been single for three months now and it's not really my ideal choice of situations but in an effort to allow myself time to heal and regroup it's what I decided I would do. Hell maybe one day somebody else will spy on me in the shower and steal my heart all over again. I joke about that now but it wasn't so funny a few months ago and you'll see what I mean as you read on.

After waiting for what seems like years I was finally done with my fifth business trip of the quarter and ready to go home. My dick throbbed at the thought of DaJuan's warm mouth milking it almost to the point of a climax and then diving into that plump, round ass. The thought of being with my lover of two years

*almost brought me joy, but sometimes I
wondered if I really made him as happy as he
makes me. Even though I took good care of him
financially, and did my best to give him all the
emotional and physical attention I could, I was
rarely home due to my job. Since I was finished
early I'd decided to surprise him with my early
arrival and a few gifts. The moment I found out
we'd be departing a couple days ahead of
schedule I called and made reservations for us
at Chef John Besh's Steakhouse and went to a
local florist and had two dozen white roses sent
to the crib along with a handwritten card
expressing my love and apologizing for being
away so much. I thought about having a limo
pick him up to meet me at the restaurant but
figured that would give the surprise away too
quickly. I'll admit I do spoil him a lot but he
deserves it, or so I thought. Plus I've never had
the opportunity to fully invest my love in anyone
and at thirty-five years old I wasn't getting any
younger and time wasn't waiting. Dr. Paul J.
Kingston III, well known book writer,
established nutrition and physical fitness
expert, adjunct professor at Loyola University,
wellness advocate, and humanitarian, all*

described me in a nutshell. 6'2, 217lbs of lean sculpted muscle, rich, velvety, milk chocolate skin, deep, hypnotizing brown eyes, shoulder length dreadlocks that I kept pulled back most of the time, and two visible tattoos that my frat brother swore would kill my chances at a thriving professional career. The one on my neck was three Chinese characters that stood for faith, love, and peace, and there was a half sleeve on my left forearm that was a mural of musical notes, microphones, and instruments. If you caught me in the gym or lounging around the house you'd probably see the others, my favorite scripture, Jeremiah 29:11, on my right pectoral, the word "blessed" painted on top of my six pack, a trio of crosses bordered by the words "saved by grace, redeemed by faith" on my back, and a tribute to my frat on my right arm. In casual encounters on the gym floor people rarely think of me as someone with a PhD and two master's degrees, but my work speaks for itself. Even though I will tell young professionals that they always need to look the part, I vowed to myself to always project an image that I felt comfortable with and made me happy. Not to mention I've never been turned away from an interview or put out of any establishments because of my appearance. Let's also not forget the fact that wrapped up in all that intellect and masculinity was an openly gay, HIV positive, black man, no I don't hide the fact that I have HIV. It's a part of my life that I wish wasn't there, but unfortunately when I was 19yrs old, a sophomore in college, I had a little problem with keeping my dick in my pants. Of course loving and wanting sex alone doesn't give you the virus, but I also had a fetish for raw sex. I mean let's be real it all feels better without the condom, but I know now that it has consequences. However, to make a long story short, in addition to being with any and everybody I also frequented sex parties, and yes I went all raw every time. So one day they were doing a health fair on campus and I decided to get tested. In my mind I had the superman complex thinking I would never catch anything, but two weeks later when the results came back I got the shock of my life. So now sixteen years later when I give my presentations or even in some conversations, like the one I had with DaJuan on our first date, I let people know and advocate hard for safe sex or even abstaining if you can hold out. I also recommend that people get tested regularly and those in relationships should go get tested together before being intimate. Even though I told DaJuan I was positive we still went to my doctor and got him tested, thankfully the results were negative. That being so I take every precaution necessary to keep them that way. Too bad he turned out to be a gold-digging hoe that I wasted a lot of my money, time, and affection on. My silly ass was so blinded by how fine he was and not to mention how good the sex was, I just let all my guards down and started going crazy over that boy.

I'll never forget the first day we met. I was taking a shower at the gym after a workout and as I was standing there I couldn't help but feel like someone was watching me. Still I proceeded to let hot water flow over my body and massage away the aches of my workout. Then after a good minute or so of that I began to lather myself up, rubbing and caressing my pumped muscles in a sort of sensuous matter. I figured if someone wanted to see my dick that bad to watch me in the shower why not give

*them a little show. Once I was all soapy I
slowly turned around and allowed the water to
rinse the suds away. While my back was turned
I thought I saw a tall, slightly toned guy
peeking around the corner at me so I decided to
turn up the heat a little. I lathered up once
again lasciviously squeezing my chest, arms,
and ass and tugging at my dick. I moaned
slightly as the sensation of self-pleasure ran
through me. I rinsed off a second time and
again soaped up my groin area before throwing
the towel over my shoulder, leaning back
against the shower wall, and giving my voyeur
an eye full of my hardening nine and a half inch
pipe. Amid all my licentious behavior I'd
inadvertently turned myself on. My moans got a
little louder with each stroke and an eruption
was eminently approaching. I lost all
cognizance of where I was as my hormones
took over leading me to a boisterous climax
that I was sure was heard out in the locker
room. As I composed myself and proceeded to
wrap up my shower I looked around cautiously
to see if I had attracted any extra attention. By
then even my little peeping tom seemed to have
fled by this point, either content with what he'd*

seen or scared off by my vociferous grunts and moans. Now finished, I turned off the water, wrapped a towel around my waist and exited the shower room. When I got to the locker where I stored my bag I noticed the guy who I thought I'd seen watching me by another locker in the corner seemingly searching for something inside. He stood at about 5'8 or 5'9, had light brown skin, bald head, a nicely toned body, and an ass that was just simply unbelievable. So if for no other reason than that I had to talk to the brother, yes I'm definitely an ass man yall, and I was mesmerized by that one.

"Hey what's up man, is this your first time here? I've never seen you around before," I called to him, attempting to start a conversation.

"Huh, uh no I've been coming here for about a month, and I've seen you on the floor a few times spotting some guys or giving advice, I thought you worked here," he responded.

"Oh nah, I'm kind of in the same profession but I work more in the private sector, I don't mind helping people though, Dr.

Kingston," I said, walking over and extending my hand, shaking with my right and handing him one of my cards with the left.

"Oh wow! Umm... I didn't expect that," he exclaimed, "But nice to meet you, I'm DaJuan and I'm a grad student at Tulane, I also bartend at Harrah's some nights to make some extra money."

"Nice to meet you as well DaJuan, and it's just habit for me to introduce myself that way, but you can just call me Paul. What are you studying at Tulane," I asked.

"Uh... social work and a little bit of psychology," he replied, looking away.

"Ok nice man, I wish you luck," I said, noticing that he was a little nervous, "By the way if you would like to join me next time I won't mind there's five shower heads in there for a reason," I laughed, walking back to my locker, pulling some lotion from my bag, and removing the towel from my waist.

"I'm sorry man, I didn't mean to spy on you, it's just when I noticed you were in there I

kind of froze up. You have a very nice d... b... body though," he replied, stammering a little as he spoke.

"So did you like what you saw in there?" I asked.

"Ummm..."

"It's ok I'm gay," I announced, noting his embarrassment and obvious fear that I would hit him or something.

"Get the fuck out of here bruh, you full of shit," he shot back.

"Nah I'm serious kid, I love men, always have since high school," I exclaimed with a smile.

"But you look like you could be a football player or something," he conceded.

"What does that mean?" I inquired.

"Nothing I guess, still I apologize to you man, that's not something I normally do," he said.

"Look you have my card, so how about you call me around eleven-thirty tomorrow and we can meet for lunch, my treat," I stated, pulling up my pants and grabbing my bag as I prepared to walk out of the locker room.

"Uh ok... I apologize again though," he answered.

"No need man, I only started jacking my dick and shit because I knew you were watching," I responded, flashing him a smile as walked out of the room.

That next day he called me, we met and talked, went on a date that Friday, had sex for the first time about three weeks after a couple more dates and a doctor visit, and here we are two years later. I boarded my flight and slept till we landed in New Orleans about two hours later. After picking up my bags I went and got my truck then I was on my way home to surprise my lover. The ride to the gated community I lived in was about a twenty-five minute drive from the airport but somehow it seemed like only five. I parked at a neighbor's house informing them that I was home early and trying to surprise DaJuan. She seemed a little uneasy when she saw me and as I walked I wondered what that was all about, but I'd deal with that later. When I got to the house I made my way around back and quietly entered through the kitchen door. The house seemed very quiet which was sort of strange so I figured that he might not have been home. This, in my mind, was good because I could do something extra special for him. So I made my way through the house and just as I was about to go up the stairs I thought I heard something in the den. Slowly, I took a few steps back and peered around the corner. Through the glass door I could see shadows moving around and heard a steady smacking sound coming from the room. I decided to get a little closer and see what was going on, but when I did I almost wished I didn't. Standing there peeking through the glass I realized that my suspicions were actually true. Right there in my den, oblivious to everything else, was DaJuan with a mouth and ass full of dick. I stood there in total shock as my heart shattered and eyes began to well with tears. Muffled moans stabbed at my eardrums and my eyes seemed to be glued to the scene of my lover being pounded from both ends. After a minute I realized that the guy's dick he was sucking was a guy I knew from the gym named Keith, but the dude fucking him was a stranger to me. I figured that this probably wasn't the trio's first time together and at this point I didn't care if it was the last, but I did know it wouldn't happen in my house again. My mind traveled back to all the times I'd called or texted him and didn't get a response or heard strange sounds while talking to him and then got rushed off the phone when I mentioned it. Every time I had been away on business, trying to provide for the man who I thought loved me was a time when this nigga had probably been doing this. The longer I stood there the initial pain and shock I felt turned to anger. "You go ahead and enjoy yourself," I said under my breath as I walked away. I quietly made my way up the stairs to my bedroom feeling more and more rage with every second that passed. Still I wasn't about to allow myself to do anything drastic, even though the 9mm locked in my safe meandered through my mind. When I got to my room I collapsed on the bed and began to cry silently. It was an emotion I'd never felt before,

14

*hurt, anger, betrayal, and malice all in one.
Never in my life had I ever been so powerfully
defenseless. There was a number of things I
could do to cause a scene and thusly be the talk
of the neighborhood and probably have my
reputation scared. All things that I didn't want
to risk, I couldn't let someone else provoke me
to shame. I looked over at the closet, then the
dresser, and lastly I peered into the bathroom
and instantly I knew what to do. I quickly rose
to my feet grabbed the two biggest suitcases I
saw and threw everything DaJuan owned inside
them. Momentarily I thought all the commotion
I was making might have been heard
downstairs but immediately dismissed the
thought and continued gathering. Within about
five minutes I had him all packed and ready to
go. I then took the bags and brought them down
to the bottom of the stairs. That's when I
noticed a few things in the kitchen and
remembered some books he had in the office. So
I grabbed the empty box I'd seen by the back
door when I came in and threw the remainder
of his stuff in it and placed it with the rest. Once
I had done this I returned to the den door and
Keith was now plowing DaJuan's ass while the*

other guy fucked his face. I'd seen Keith in the shower a few times and he had a real nicely toned body, but I didn't know he was such a grower. I laughed to myself watching his long red dick slide in and out as he stroked and in the midst of that laugh my eyes met with his and there was an immediate panic that flushed over his face.

Chapter 2

Cutting You Off

"Nah, nah don't worry about me, yall go head and fuck the shit out of that nigga," I said announcing my presence to DaJuan and the other guy who had just began to explode all over DaJuan's lips, "Just make sure you take him with you when you're done. All his shit is packed and waiting by the stairs, and I'll see you at the gym tomorrow Keith," I said nonchalantly as I walked off.

Moments later, in true cheater fashion, DaJuan comes running after me. Adorned with all the dramatics of how sorry he was and a bunch of other mess about how he got so lonely while I was away that I wasn't trying to hear. Far as I was concerned the damage had been done and there wasn't anything to discuss.

"Paul... baby... please just let me explain... it's not what it looks..."

"Seriously...you can't be that stupid to say what I think you were about to say," I snapped, cutting him off and turning to face him.

"Ok, but I..."

"You have nothing else to say to me kid, and if you haven't noticed your ride is about to leave you. Oh and don't bother trying to use your phone, credit card, or gym membership, and don't even think about coming back here," I barked coldly, cutting him off again, "Keith do me a favor and take this bitch toy with you," I continued, directing my attention my gym partner as he came out the room, "Don't worry I don't have no beef with you, just get this trash out of my house before I burn it," I added in a soothingly malicious tone.

"Sure Paul, I'll see you around at the gym," he replied.

"Paul..."

"Come on D, I've known Paul long enough to know that he's not gonna change his mind and frankly bruh you just shitted and stepped in it so let's just go," Keith reasoned, taking DaJuan by the arm.

"Bye!" I called behind them.

I sat there that day, at my desk just looking at the computer screen, still angry but somewhat at peace knowing that I didn't have to worry about my heart being trampled or any further frivolous use of my credit cards and checking account. It was almost surreal to me that this had actually happened, but in a way I was glad it did. I mean who falls in love with a guy you catch watching you in the shower at the gym? Wait I know, that dumb, overly emotional dude they call Paul Kingston. So afraid that I was going to grow old and gray and never experience what it was like to be in love I just jumped in the pool head first in my twenty-five hundred dollar Versace suit. Now two years later I'm sitting here in my home office with a broken heart and nothing but a trail of tears and receipts to show for my pain. The icing on the cake though is that I did all I did for the dude and it ain't really mean anything. I'll admit the sex got me hooked first, but as time went on and I thought I was getting to know DaJuan I started falling for him. The more I saw him push and strive for better the more feelings I felt. I was in love with the idea of loving and something in me just wanted to take care of him. I guess I saw something in him that he didn't see in his self, maybe it was a little of me I saw in him. You know I started from basically nothing, but I worked my ass off to get through school, held down two jobs to pay for what my scholarships didn't cover, and invested a good portion of the extra money in a savings account, and look at me now. I've got all the accoutrements of a thriving young professional and I'm still rising higher. Early on in the relationship DaJuan and I talked about our dreams, our goals, and planned steps to get us to where we wanted to be. He seemed to have the same drive and hunger for success as me, juggling work and school, always hungry for a break or opportunity to advance while on the road to glory. Aside from the sex being good, these are the things that made me fall for him and as his man I wanted to alleviate the struggle a little. So like a fool I spoiled the hell out of him, but in retrospect I can now see how he was basically just using me. Sitting there at that desk that day I cried, I got angry, and I felt the hurt of heartbreak and betrayal for the very first time. For hours I just sulked and plotted and then retreated in my thoughts to take the high road instead of getting even. Then I got a text from Keith saying he wanted to talk to me but I refused to answer. Even though I really had no issue with him in my mind there was still a bruise on my heart inflicted by people I'd trusted. The very people that I had allowed myself to be vulnerable around had turned on me. So at that moment I didn't want to be bothered but thirty minutes later he called and left a voicemail which I listened to and then just deleted. Then after another fifteen minutes he called again. This time, reluctantly, I answered.

"Paul I know it's some shit going through your head right now but please just listen to me for a minute," Keith blurted out before I could even get the word hello out of my mouth.

"Ok, go head and say what you feel you need to say," I replied.

"First off I didn't know you and dude were together like that. I saw y'all work out together sometimes and since I knew you were gay I figured you might have got some head from him or been fucking that nigga but never thought y'all had anything past that. Shit even today when he invited me and Brian over I ain't know that was your house we were coming to.

You know we workout together and talk a good bit but we've never really got too personal so I was shocked to find out that the man that was hardly home was you," he explained.

"I already told you I don't have no beef with you so you ain't got to worry bruh, I'm not mad at you," I stated calmly.

"Yea you did but when I saw you today there was something in your eyes that was real familiar to me. You walked in and saw your friend fucking your lover and I know that shit hurt you bruh. On the outside you were the typical apathetic guy that I'd gotten to know over the years but your eyes told a different story," he continued, then taking a brief pause, "Shit if I had known something sooner I would had said something to you bruh," he added.

"Said something like what," I asked.

"Well I'm kind of sure you have an idea now but DaJuan ain't wifey material bruh and I'm sure today ain't the first time he done had other niggas in your house. The muthafucka was too calm even though he told us you were

out of town, it was a vibe like, it's ok yall I do this shit all the time," Keith said.

"Yea I kind of had my thoughts about that when I saw what was going down," I concurred, finally picking myself up from the desk and heading upstairs.

"Yea, I felt a lil uneasy about it but my dick felt something else you dig," he laughed, in an attempt to lighten the moment I guess.

"I can imagine it did and yo ass is packing more than I thought you were," I joked, "but I still have a dinner reservation for tonight, it was planned for DaJuan and I but why don't you join me and we can talk some more," I added.

"You really asking me to go somewhere with you Dr. Kingston," he asked in surprise.

"Is that a problem bruh," I answered.

"Nah but shit you ain't ask me to go nowhere in the nearly five years I've known you," Keith stated.

"Ok well that changes tonight, and it's my treat," I replied.

"You not gon tell me you need an annulment or some kind of legal work done are you? When my clients treat me to something it's normally followed by some kind of service being needed," he laughed.

"You know I forgot you were a lawyer bruh, but nah, I just need to get out the house and since everything is already paid for why not have somebody come with me," I suggested coyly.

"Ok, but I'll meet you there and I'll handle the tip," he said, seemingly not understanding what I'm treating meant.

"Nah you ain't got to drive just give me your address, I'll send the car for you, and we can discuss who pays the tip when the time comes," I said.

"Ok, ok where are we are going and what time should I be ready," Keith inquired.

"Just get dressed and the car will be there to get you once you give me the address," I reiterated impatiently.

"Aight man, 3948 King Azeri Lane," he answered.

"Thank you sir," I laughed, *"The car will be there to get you in bout thirty minutes so be ready,"* I added.

"Thirty minutes bruh... aight then... let me get off this phone so I can be ready," he replied, obviously restraining the irritation of being told at the last minute.

"Ok see you later," I laughed before hanging up.

Chapter 3

Dinner Date

About thirty-five minutes later I was sitting in a booth at the restaurant waiting for Keith to arrive. My mind raced at the thought of what else he could have to tell me. On one hand I wanted to know but then on the other I wasn't sure if I was ready to hear any more about how much of a fool I had been. Still the truth of the matter was I was there now and whatever else needed to be said would be said and that was all. I was also a little excited to actually be on a little "date" with my boy since I had never really seen him anywhere but in the gym. As pathetic as it may have sounded, he was absolutely right about not knowing much about me past what I do for a living and the small talk we have about sports and current events during our workouts together. So I anxiously sat there in my booth watching the door as I waited for him to get there. It was pretty quiet even for a Wednesday night and that made me extra antsy. Every time I saw someone come past the bar I was stretching my neck as far out of my dimly lit corner as I could in anticipation. Then finally, about fifteen minutes late, he made his arrival.

"Hey man I'm sorry about the delay, the driver got lost and since he didn't have a contact number for me he had to stop and ask for directions. I was a little glad he took longer than expected cause I didn't know what to put on so I wasn't dressed at the time he was supposed to be there. Hell even when I got in the car I still wasn't sure if I had on the right thing but I just did a business casual look so I wouldn't be too underdressed or overdressed," Keith explained as the hostess showed him to his seat.

"It's ok man I was a little behind myself, but I'm glad you came," I replied.

"Did I really have a choice," he inquired.

"Of course you did," I said.

"Well in that case... excuse me can somebody flag down that car that just let me out," Keith announced just loud enough for the nearest waitress to hear him before falling out in laughter at his self.

"Is there something wrong sir," the young lady asked.

"No, no everything is fine maim I was just joking with my friend here," Keith explained, pointing to me.

"See you causing a scene already, I'm kind of glad I didn't ever take you anywhere with me," I laughed as the young waitress rolled her eyes and walked away.

"Man I know how to act I just wanted to make you laugh a little, plus it's hardly anybody in here," he said.

"Yea ok well it's good to see you with clothes on," I joked.

"Is it really? I thought you liked what you saw," Keith commented with a smile.

"Well that depends on how you define like, but what I said was I didn't know you had that much dick," I answered, *"I've seen you naked probably more times than what should be allowed between friends,"* I added.

"You know what, I'm a just let that subject rest right there and you know there is no way I'm a let you pick up this tab by yourself," he replied.

"Yea you do that and why not," I asked.

"Dude we're at Besh Steakhouse, really? Shit if I let you spend this much money on me I might have to give you some service," Keith stated looking at me with a soft, seductive glare in his eyes.

"Whatever bruh, you probably just want to lend me your services anyway," I snapped, glaring back at him.

"Ok once again, I'm a leave that that alone. How the hell are you tonight brother," he said, changing the subject.

"Ha, ha what's wrong Keith I ain't used to you backing down so much," I asked.

"I'm just chilling, I ain't used to seeing you anywhere but the gym so I'm taking time to indulge in the moment," he answered shyly.

"Man don't give me that quiet school girl act," I said, turning my brow and picking up the menu.

"Hey guys I'm Michelle and I'll be your waitress this evening can I start y'all off with something to drink," the waitress chirped as she approached the table.

"Actually sweetheart let me get an order of barbeque shrimp to start off and some lemonade. Keith you know what you want," I asked pushing the spotlight on him.

"Ummm... to be honest I've never been here so ummm... help me out bro," he answered with a confused look on his face.

"Well what do you like? For appetizers we have oysters, a couple trios, stuffed crab shells, and the shrimp that your friend just ordered. We also have soups and salads if you don't want any of the other stuff," Michelle chimed in cheerfully.

"I still don't know, but you can bring me some lemonade as well. Maybe by the time you

get back with the drinks I should have made a decision, " Keith replied.

"Ok take your time honey, and I'll go get your drinks," she stated as she walked away.

"Dude you kidding right? You've really never been here," I asked.

"Nah I'm serious, I've been to John Besh's other spots but yea never this one," he answered, dipping his head.

"No need to be ashamed bruh, shit the steakhouse and the buffet over there are the only reasons I come to Harrah's, not to mention when DaJuan was with me we used to get a discount," I laughed.

"Excuse me, I'm a little embarrassed but my friend over there and I have been watching you guys since you came in here. He didn't want to come over here so I said I'd come talk to you instead," a young woman said, "I hope you don't think I'm crazy but we just thought you two were very attractive," she added, blushing a little as she spoke.

"It's a little strange but I'm actually flattered," Keith said.

"Yea I'm a little impressed by the gesture myself," I added.

"Well we made a little bet before I walked over," she stated shyly.

"Here are your drinks my darlings, I'll give yall a bit longer, then come back for your appetizer orders," Michelle announced sitting the drinks on the table, *"Will you be joining them maim,"* she inquired, turning her attention to the young woman standing on the other side of the table.

"Oh no, my friend and I are sitting over there, I just came over to tell them about the bet at the office," the woman said.

"Ok well fellas I'll be around just flag me over when you're ready to order," Michelle said as she walked off.

"So what's this bet," I asked.

"I don't want to say this too loud," the woman began, beckoning for us to come closer,

"if I suck both of your dicks while he watches he'll pick up the tab for all our meals," she continued just above a whisper once we were close enough.

"Whoa... say what?" Keith and I sang in unison.

"So what happens if you don't," Keith asked.

"I have to pay for our meals and deal with the embarrassment of looking like a fool for approaching you guys," she answered.

"I see well, what you think we should do bruh? You think we should help this sexy lil Latina out," Keith asked.

"I don't know she said it was a bet, do you really want to suck our dicks shawty," I inquired keeping my eyes on her.

"And what's your name sexy," Keith chimed in before she could answer the first question.

"I'm a lil nervous about it, but ummm... my name is Clarissa," she answered.

"Well Clarissa I'm working with about 9.5 inches and my boy just as big. You think you can handle that," I asked.

"I'm about 10 maybe 10.5 inches," Keith added.

"Ummm... I don't know but I'm willing to try, plus I mean it's a free meal in it for all of us," Clarissa giggled nervously.

"Put your hand in my lap and feel around a bit baby girl, then tell me if you still feel brave," Keith instructed.

Chapter 4

Bet On It

"What you say we up the stakes a bit," I suggested.

"What do you mean," she questioned.

"Let's say we raise the bet a little, instead of just sucking our dicks, how bout we fuck you, your voyeur friend buys us all dinner, and pays me and Keith $50 a piece," I said, watching her eyes grow wide as she felt on Keith's dick and then looked back at the table where her friend was sitting and watching.

"Ummm... wow, let me go talk to him and see what he says," Clarissa stammered a little, swallowing hard as she spoke.

"You like what you feel down there sweetie," Keith asked.

"Honestly, I'm curious to see it and I'd like to feel yours too, but let me go talk to Jules and I'll be back," she said, anxiously looking back and forth from Keith, to me, back at Jules, and again to Keith and me.

"Ok you go do that," I said, beckoning for Michelle.

"I don't think he'll have a problem with throwing out a lil extra to see a lil more, but I'll be back," Clarissa said as she walked away.

"That nervous act seemed a bit fake to me bruh," I said once she was out of ear's reach.

"Yea I was thinking that too son. The way she was pulling on my dick I'm sure she's been round the hood a few times," Keith laughed.

"So my darlings are yall ready to order," Michelle asking gently placing a hand on my shoulder as she approached the table.

"I was ready the first time ma, we were waiting on Mr. First over there," I joked, looking up at the elderly white lady.

"Oh hush boy, baby are you ready to order yet," she asked scolding me with a tap on the arm and turning her attention to Keith.

"Yes maim I think I'll just have the 'Louisiana Three Way' and would it be possible

for my oysters to be fried extra crispy instead of the cocktail," he answered respectfully.

"Sure thing honey and you want the spicy ranch dressing that comes with it," she inquired.

"Ummm if I can still get the cocktail sauce I'll take that but if not yea I guess," Keith stated.

"Absolutely sweetie and you wanted the BBQ shrimp right Mr. Man," she stated, glaring at me over her glasses.

"Yes main," I answered.

"Ok I'll go put this in and get you guys a refill on those drinks. Your food should be out in about ten or fifteen minutes my darlings," Michelle said before leaving us once again.

"So you think ole girl gon come back bruh," Keith asked, slurping up the last of his lemonade.

"I don't..."

"Hey I'm back," Clarissa announced, cutting me off, but literally answering Keith's question for me, "Jules said that's cool, but he wants a DP with the bigger of the two of you in my ass and he'll pay yall a hundred bucks a piece," she added, seemingly a lot bolder now than she was before she walked away.

"It's fine with me, you down Paul," Keith replied, throwing the ball to me.

"Are you sure you want to do this," I asked solemnly, looking directly in her eyes.

"If I can be honest... I never took two dicks inside me before but I'm sure it'll be fun," she responded with a smile.

"Humm... ok that ain't the answer I expected but shit if that's how you feel why don't you come taste my dick right now," I said, attempting to test her limits.

"Right here at the table," she gasped.

"Yea why not, then you can come do mine," Keith interjected.

"Unless you're afraid that somebody will see you," I taunted.

"Are you serious," she laughed nervously.

"I mean if you're scared we can just call the whole bet off and forget this ever happened," Keith added.

"I'm just saying we got to know if it's worth our wild," I stated nonchalantly.

"But you're..."

"Yea I know your friend offered to pay for our dinner, but I make plenty money and so does my friend so we ain't in need of no handouts," I interrupted before she could even bring it up again.

"In other words sweetheart we need to know if you can actually suck dick before we agree and if you can't then we ain't fucking you," Keith said coldly.

"Mumm... that's kind of risky but... take it out and let me show you," she said hesitantly

with a funny little giggle and moan mixed together and a devilish grin on her face.

"Come on over here," I ordered, discreetly unzipping my pants and pulling my dick out.

"Mumm I'm kind of getting wet already," Clarissa said, sliding next to me in the booth.

"Let me feel that shit, bring yo ass in the middle," Keith barked, jumping up and roughly pulling her around the other side of the table.

"Oh damn baby," she shrieked in surprise.

"Seem like you like that rough shit," I laughed, looking around to see if we had attracted any attention.

"I think she do bruh," Keith chuckled, "Lay your head down in his lap bitch," he snapped at her before taking his seat again.

"Mumm damn papi... you got a nice dick," Clarissa exclaimed.

"Don't just look at it suck it," I retorted, smacking my meat against her lips.

"Yea she loving this shit dawg, this fucking pussy getting wet like a... fuck ma lift that leg up a little," Keith yelped diving down behind her and spreading her ass open before I could blink an eye.

"Damn this hoe ain't got no panties on," I noted as I watched Keith run his finger through the crack of her ass and then flicking his tongue over her clit.

"Mumm, mumm, mumm," she moaned taking my hardening dick as far as she could into her mouth.

"How that head feeling bruh," Keith asked a few moments later, sitting back up after his quick snack.

"Kind of good honestly, but the test will be if she can get this gay man's dick hard," I laughed, *"How was the fish,"* I added.

"Sweet my nigga and from the looks of it she doing a good job," Keith answered, peering over into my lap.

"Yea I'm surprised, she's making progress bruh," I laughed feeling a bit weird getting head from a female and enjoying it.

"Well shit, I hope she gets to the goal because I want to feel that shit too before somebody comes," he cried.

"She was doing it best when you were eating her pussy," I replied suggestively.

"Ha, ha as much as I want to you know I can't stay down there," he laughed.

"Shit she just took me to the balls son," I exclaimed, "the last bitch that gave me head could only get about half in her mouth," I continued, obviously intrigued and a little turned on by the skill she was showing.

"Well it's a good thing we back here in this corner and she ducked off under the table, but then again if they seat somebody at any of these tables in front of us that's a wrap... damn

this shit getting wetter bruh," Keith said wiggling his fingers inside her.

"Fuck, suck that dick ma," I growled, pushing her head down in my lap as she moaned from the feeling of Keith's fingers teasing her pussy.

"Yo somebody is coming," Keith alerted just as my dick got rock solid.

"Hi guys, I'm Linda the manager on duty tonight and I just wanted to personally come over and tell you that we apologize for the inconvenience but there was a little incident in the kitchen and as a result they are a little backlogged at the moment but your appetizers will be out as soon as possible. Ummm... is she ok," the lady paused noticing how Clarissa was leaned over between us.

"Yes I'm fine, I was just trying to wipe the lemonade off his pants before it made a stain," Clarissa chirped popping up from her position.

"Ok... well... as I was saying your orders will be out soon but on the behalf of the

restaurant I want to offer you both a free appetizer for your next visit with us," Linda continued, seeming not to buy Clarissa's story.

"You said there was an accident or something in the kitchen, is everyone ok," I asked, covering my dick as best I could with my jacket.

"Yes sir, it was just a little minor fall that just so happened to knock a bunch of orders on the floor, so our employee is ok but the food obviously didn't survive," she joked.

"Ok so about how much longer will it be," Keith inquired.

"At most, maybe another thirty minutes because they had to start everything over again, but no worries I will personally see to you guys being taken care of and Michelle will be over periodically as well to make sure things are going well and again I apologize and I hope you guys have a great evening," she assured us before leaving the table.

Once Linda was out of sight and the coast was clear Clarissa got back to work on my dick. I still couldn't believe that a woman was giving me a nice ass blowjob. The last time I was with a female was when I was a sophomore in college. It's actually probable that a woman gave me HIV, but being as much of a hoe as I was there's no way to tell for sure. Still it was part of the reason I started dealing with men exclusively. This one right here though reminded me a lil bit of what sex with a woman was like as she moaned and sucked the hell out my dick. I honestly almost forgot where we were when she took me all the way into her throat again, but was quickly reminded by Keith begging for his turn. So we went ahead and switched around so he could get his dick sucked while I sheepishly felt around on her ass. It was almost comical how I fumbled around back there like a virgin, but eventually I found my groove. Sadly we were interrupted by our food being brought out, which wasn't a bad thing since we came there to eat.

"Hey my darlings so sorry it took so long but here we are," Michelle announced as she sat the tray with our plates down beside the table.

*"Well I guess I'll see you guys later,"
Clarissa said, quickly hoping up when she saw
Michelle had arrived.*

*"Yea we will definitely catch up with you
and Jules later," I called behind her.*

*"Ok, I'll be looking forward to it," she
turned and said with a smile.*

*"That girl was over here bothering you
boys again," Michelle asked as she sat our
plates down in front of us.*

*"No maim, we were just talking about
the bet and I hope we win this time," Keith
answered politely.*

*"Ok, well baby I'll be back shortly for
your entrée orders, unless yall are ready now,"
she replied.*

*"Oh no, we should be ready when you
get back though," I answered.*

*"Ok well I'll give yall some time and I'll
be back," Michelle stated before leaving us.*

Chapter 5

Turned Out

"*I don't know about you bruh, but I'm not really hungry,*" *I said, gazing over at Clarissa and Jules ordering their food.*

"*Shit I'll eat for you bruh,*" *Keith laughed,* "*But from the way you looking back at them people I think you might have another meal in mind and I can tell you that that's a way to work up an appetite,*" *he continued jokingly.*

"*I'm kind of intrigued by that idea but I sort of lost my appetite when I walked in my house and found two niggas fucking my dude,*" *I stated, taking a small bite of one of the huge shrimp I had,* "*This shit is good though bruh,*" *I added.*

"*Let me try one of them and you can taste these oysters or a piece of this,*" *he said pointing to the crab cake,* "*But Paul honestly bruh, if I had known you and dude were together I...*"

"*Keith you don't have to man and yea give me a bite of that,*" *I interjected, cutting him off and reaching across the table for a fork full of his crab cake.*

51

*"Paul can I just say one thing though,"
Keith inquired hesitantly.*

"You just did nigga," I laughed.

"Come on man for real," he replied.

"Yea sure go ahead bruh," I said.

*"Well I told you on the phone that
DaJuan was pretty much a hoe, but I have to
admit that today wasn't my first time fucking
him, I'd never been in your house before, but he
had been to my crib a few times and we messed
around in the shower at the gym a couple times
too. There were times when we were together
and his phone would ring or something and
he'd tell me I got to take this and he'd be
talking while I was eating his ass or even
fucking him," Keith began informing me.*

*"Oh really," I said making mental note
of what I was being told and recollecting times
when I talked to DaJuan and he was too
breathless too talk.*

*"Yea man I used to think that shit was
aggravating but I figured it must be important if*

he got to answer that shit in the middle of us getting it in," he continued.

"So when exactly did you meet DaJuan or maybe I should ask when did yall start fucking," I asked.

"Well the first time was sort of awkward," he replied, pausing for a moment to swallow his food and take a sip of his drink, "I actually caught the nigga spying on me in the shower. He had come up to me while I was working out asking me questions about how I got my body so toned and if I had ever taken any supplements or whatever. I remembered seeing him with you a couple times so I figured he was cool and I entertained him for a while, showed him a few things. Then he went on bout his business, but when I got in the shower I just had this feeling that somebody was watching me. So I played it cool thinking maybe I'm just imagining it till I actually saw him peeking from around the corner. When our eyes met he dashed off and instinctively I went after him. My first thought was to beat his ass but once I caught him I got a lil curious and decided to bully him a bit and see how far I could take it.

So I decided to pull his ass back into the shower, mind you I'm but ass naked and dripping wet. Could have busted my black ass trying to run after somebody but shit I caught that nigga," he laughed continuing his story.

"Humm this sounds vaguely familiar, except for the chase, but tell me more," I stated.

"Well once we were back in the shower I roughed him up a bit and then shoved him on the floor. I could see the fear in his eyes and that kind of gave me a bit of an adrenaline rush. So I started talking shit to him, grabbing my dick, shaking it at him, making him sniff my musty balls and ass. Then something clicked in my head and without thinking commanded him to suck my dick. I remember saying some shit like, 'you like it enough to spy on it now suck it,' or something like that, but I didn't really expect to get what I got. Within moments of him taking my shit in his mouth I was rock hard and that surprised the fuck out of me because I had never had my dick sucked by a dude before," Keith continued.

"Wait what you mean you never got head from a dude before?" I asked, surprised by his statement.

"I'd never done it before, that was the first time," he admitted.

"Hello my sweeties are y'all ready for your next course," Michelle asked.

"Yea I think I'll have the 12oz Berkshire pork chop and my friend will have the 14oz seared rib eye," I answered.

"Ok... now baby is that really what you want or us he just speaking for you to speed things up," she inquired, turning her attention to Keith.

"The beef and fries are good with me," he laughed, "But can I get another refill on this please," he added.

"Sure thing honey," Michelle said, playfully rolling her eyes at me and walking away.

"I think she's sweet on you bruh, rubbing your shoulder, cracking jokes, alright Dr. Kingston got him a cougar," Keith laughed.

"Well I'm sorry to disappoint her but once again I'm gay! I like men," I exclaimed proudly.

"Seem like you got a lil bit of straightness in you to me," Keith stated.

"What you mean? I'm always gon be masculine bruh," I shot back curiously.

"Nah I don't mean that I'm talking about when Clarissa was sucking yo dick. It seemed like you was enjoying that shit to me my nigga," he said.

"I ain't saying I've never fucked a woman. They just ain't my preferred cup of tea anymore," I replied.

"Ok, ok I got you bruh! So what do you plan to do about that bet," Keith asked, grabbing for another one of my shrimp.

"I guess we'll have to deal with that when the situation comes, if she comes back.

That bitch saw Michelle and bolted out like she had seen the warden, and don't fuck with my plate again nigga," I said sternly, smacking his hand away.

"I thought we were sharing yo," Keith exclaimed.

"You asked for one and I gave you one now back up son," I laughed.

"Aight man, my bad," he stated.

"Uh huh, now finish telling me the story bruh," I said impatiently.

"Well he started sucking my dick and that shit felt amazing bruh! You know when I said suck my dick I didn't think I was gon really get my dick sucked," he blurted out excitedly.

"But if you told him to do it, what you mean," I laughed.

"Like I ain't think he was gon know how, but that nigga started sucking, my shit got rock, and I just grabbed him by the head and started trying to choke that nigga with it. However, the funny thing was even when I was basically

slapping his face with my balls that nigga still wouldn't gag. Like he was deep throating my shit son! It ain't even feel like a mouth bruh. It felt like I was in some wet ass fuckin pussy! So I was like fuck this nigga doing me better than my bitch and that blew my fuckin mind yo," Keith explained.

"Yea that nigga was one of the best dick suckers I ever met," I concurred.

"For real though, I was expecting him to be all nervous, licking it and just barely putting the head in his mouth, but homie took my shit down like a pro bruh. So I started getting more aggressive, ramming my dick down his throat, smacking his face, pinching his nipples and punching his chest, and he seemed to be loving that shit. Then I remember this chick licking my ass one time and it was sort of interesting you dig. So in my head I'm like I'm a make this muthafucka lick my ass," he chuckled, "Dude he started doing that shit and my head was gone! I think I even forgot where I was for about two or three minutes bruh," he added.

"*Nigga you crazy, but you said this was your first time ever doing something with a dude,*" *I asked.*

"*Yea, I ain't bullshiting bruh.*" *Keith declared.*

"*So what the hell made you do it? Because I honestly thought you were straight then I get to my house today and find you and chocolate Hercules fucking the shit out of DaJuan. Did you think any of this through or did you even... like... what was going through you head son,*" *I interrogated, trying to pick his brain a little.*

"*Paul I don't even know. Initially I was pissed and ready to beat this nigga's ass for spying on me, but then it's like something else took over. I saw him down there on the floor and instead of hurting him I thought I would humiliate him. That's when I made him sniff my balls and shit, but since he did that with no hesitation I wanted to test him a lil more. You know it ain't like I just assumed this nigga gay, he suck dick, I'm a make him suck my dick, then I'm a make him eat my ass, and then fuck him in the ass. I think if I had really thought it through I would probably stuck with my first mind, beat his ass, and left him on the floor in the shower,"* he answered.

"*So you fucked him too,"* I gasped on amazement.

"*Yea son, and that shit was... oh my God yo! I would have never imagined fucking a dude would feel like that. I had never even fucked any of my bitches in the ass so it was a whole new experience for me,"* he replied.

"*Damn you really turned yourself out huh,"* I joked.

"*You know in a way I kind of did,"* he laughed, "*but to answer your question I guess my whole thought process was this nigga violated me watching me in the shower so I'm a pay his ass back by violating him,"* he stated.

"*I feel that, I mean even if you do suck dick or whatever, the fact of somebody constraining you puts a whole new spin on the situation,"* I reasoned.

"Right, right and I honestly believe that was my intent, but in trying to humiliate him I got caught up and started enjoying the shit. Then to be honest I think he was really feeling all that kinky shit too. I didn't let him know I was loving it too, at least not that day, so after I busted on his face I just shoved him to the side, finished my shower, and left. So then the next time I saw him I took advantage of that ass again and we continued like that for about a month, but that last time I brought my nigga Brian, or chocolate Hercules like you called him, in for some extra fun. The thing I didn't know though was that nigga Brian had been fucking DaJuan for months before I even touched him. So when I called his name and he came joined us in the locker room that day my lil game was over and for the last maybe four months or so we just been fucking. Sometimes Brain or another guy from the gym or... wait a minute... aye don't I know you son," Keith said stopping midsentence as he noticed a stocky, light skinned dude passing our table.

Chapter 6

Flirt or Thot

"Huh... oh umm... yea I think we met at a party right," the guy said, stopping and turning to acknowledge Keith.

"Yea your name is Mike right?" Keith inquired.

"Micah... but umm... who's your friend," he asked, smiling at me.

"This is my gym partner Paul," Keith answered, introducing me.

"So are his muscles the only thing big on him," Micah asked, boldly rubbing my arm.

"Very straight forward huh son," I said, catching his hand and pulling him down into the booth. Obviously caught off guard by my reaction, he started to fall face first and would've hit the table if I hadn't caught him.

"I don't think... "

"Nah, nah Keith, he wanted to know something about me so let's give him a chance to find out," I snapped, cutting Keith off.

"Oh really, I can find out huh my nigga," Micah inquired, making his self a little comfortable in my arms.

"Yea go ahead and see bruh," I replied nonchalantly, laying back and pulling him in closer to me.

"Ok," he said, wasting no time sliding his hand into my pants and grabbing hold of my dick.

"Umm... I think you might want to sit up before somebody comes," Keith warned, looking around nervously.

"Nah he said I could find out what I wanted to know," Micah said.

"Uh huh and since you feeling on me I'm a feel on you," I said, grabbing a handful of his thick ass.

"Yo we in the public y'all," Keith exclaimed, getting more and more nervous by the minute.

"Say bruh just chill, you wasn't tripping when ole girl was over here, so relax cause you

know I'm a share with you nigga," I said sternly, "Damn this ass is soft son," I continued turning my attention back to Micah.

"It feels better on the inside, and I don't plan to just feel on you," he replied, pushing my hand inside his jeans and then unzipping my pants.

"Well I ain't stopping you bruh, do you," I stated as my finger found its way to his moist hole.

"I will," Micah answered, finally succeeding at pulling my dick out after a brief struggle.

"So I guess I'm playing lookout now huh," Keith stated sarcastically.

"That would be nice of you," I moaned, slipping two fingers into Micah's ass as he slid his lips down on my semi erect dick.

"Yea the last thing we need is somebody to walk by or come over and see him laid over in your lap. Not too sure if we'll be able to explain that," Keith whined.

"Well that's why we got you watching, so we don't get caught right," Micah responded, catching a quick breath before taking my dick back into the back of his throat.

"So yall ganging up on me right... ok... and I see you really do like men more," Keith stated peering into my lap and noticing how quickly I got hard from Micah sucking me off.

"I told you that, and in my opinion he sucks dick better than her," I replied.

"This ass probably better than her pussy too," Micah chimed in.

"Let me find out," I laughed.

"Paul, are you serious nigga," Keith asked nervously.

"I mean he came looking, so why not give it to him," I replied.

"Oh so you just bout to put that dick in me huh son," Micah laughed.

"Fucking right, you ain't scared is you nigga," I answered, pushing him over and

sliding up out of the booth with my dick hanging out, "Slid over nigga," I ordered, gently pushing him.

"I ain't scared of shit nigga," Micah snapped back.

"Paul... you sure you thinking clearly bruh," Keith asked.

"My mind is as clear as it's ever been my dude, pull them pants down and lay on your side son," I instructed, sitting back down.

"Well my pants are down nigga so what you gon do," Micah scoffed.

"He ain't gon do nothing because here come Michelle now," Keith interposed.

"Shit," I cried irritably.

"Well I'm out of here," Micah stated, pulling his pants up and sitting upright.

"Hold on a sec," I said, reaching into my coat pocket, "Get at me later," I added handing him one of my business cards.

"Humm, Dr. Kingston huh... oh umm... Keith are you coming to our party this weekend," Micah inquired, sliding pass me.

"Umm... I'm not sure yet, where's it gonna be," he asked.

"I think it'll be at a hotel, but I don't know if DaJuan has locked in a reservation yet. When I talked to him about an hour ago he seemed a little agitated bout something, but I had to meet a potential client here so we didn't talk long," Micah answered.

"He was agitated huh," I chuckled.

"Yea, I don't know what his issue was but I'll find out later, you know him too," Micah asked.

"Uh yea, they've met," Keith exclaimed.

"Yea we chill when I'm in town," I added with a sly grin on my face.

"Humm ok... maybe you should come to the party too. I'm sure DaJuan and the rest of the bottoms wouldn't mind meeting up with you," he stated.

"I'll think about it bruh," I laughed.

"What's funny," Micah inquired, perplexed by my reaction.

"He's just flattered that you offered that's all," Keith interjected before I could answer.

"Excuse me sweetie," Michelle said, making her way around Micah, *"I got y'all some refills and your plates should be out shortly my darlings. Is there anything else I can get for y'all,"* she added.

"Uh... when you come back we'll be ready to order dessert, but we'll probably take that to go," I answered.

"Ok hun, I'll be right back with your entrées," she chirped.

"Well I'll be in touch doc, I have an early appointment in the morning, but hopefully I'll see both of y'all at the party," Micah stated, making his exit.

"Ok, I'll see you around," Keith said.

Chapter 7

Check Please

About five minutes later Michelle returned with our food and Keith and I discussed more of his exploits with DaJuan. It turns out that they had been messing around for about four months, but Keith definitely wasn't the only one. How the hell I'd been so blind to everything was sort of disconcerting. Then again when you think about how much I was working, traveling, and just being completely engrossed in my career it wasn't all that hard to see. I had sort of neglected him but in lieu of spending time with him I spoiled him with lavish gifts. Beyond our first two months we might have had sex a handful of times outside of the special occasions like anniversary and birthdays. So maybe I did play my part in pushing him to do what he did. Still it hurts to invest so much in someone, give them your trust, give them your heart, and then find out what you thought you had was a lie.

"Hey fellas is everything going ok," Linda asked.

"Uh yea... I think whatever was said to that guy after he dropped that pan on floor made everybody step their game up," I laughed.

"Yea everything's been real good," Keith added.

"Wonderful, I'm glad to hear that the evening turned out well for you guys. Remember my name is Linda and if you need anything please don't hesitate to ask for me. Enjoy the rest of your evening," she replied and walked off.

"Hey you want to have a glass of wine," I asked out of the blue as I took the last sips of my lemonade.

"Wine, twenty minutes ago you was about to fuck a nigga right here in the booth. In the middle of the dining room you was about to fuck some dude that just asked you a question. I admit he was a bit forward, but I don't think the nigga was asking for the dick right here on the spot," Keith replied.

"He ain't object to getting it either," I stated coldly.

"No he didn't, and knowing him he wouldn't, that's one of DaJuan's best friends. You know they say birds of a feather flock

together... but... Paul I think I understand where you are right now and I want you to know I'm here for you bruh. It's awkward as hell because... well you already know why, but you are my friend. Shit this is our first time sitting down and talking but after all these years I feel like we have some kind of relationship and I honestly enjoy the time we spend together. Now before you say it I already know I'm blabbing, preaching, fussing whatever, I'd love to have a drink with you but are you sure you can handle it right now," he said, looking me square in the eyes.

"Shit I'm kind of speechless now bruh, but uh... yea man I'm good for it. True I was about to do something I would have probably regretted later but you know when Clarissa was over here you ain't object to my crazy ideas either," I answered, "Is it warm in here to you," I added, slipping out of my jacket.

"I'm a lil hot in other ways, but it's comfortable in here to me, and you're right I didn't. That was my moment of insanity," Keith laughed.

"So if I had told Mr. Loose Draws to suck yo dick too you would have been cool right," I joked.

"Man, I ain't even bout to entertain that. Go ahead and order the wine bruh," Keith answered, gulping down the last of his lemonade.

"Uh excuse me could you call Michelle, our waitress, please," I asked the server that was passing by us.

"Yes sir, I'll go get her for you as soon as I deliver these appetizers," the young man said.

"Never mind here she comes," I called after him.

"You looking for me handsome," Michelle asked as she approached the table.

"Yea, even though we're about halfway through the course already can we see a wine list," I asked.

"Sure, I have one right here, do you need a minute to look over it or do you have an idea of what you want already. Also keep in mind

that our selections can also be purchased by the glass," she replied, handling me the list as requested.

"Umm I think I have a pretty good idea, let me get two glasses of Pinot Grigio for me and I guess merlot..."

"Hold on a sec, let me see it... come on let me see," Keith interjected, cutting me off.

"Oh give it to him tight pants," Michelle stated, pulling it from my hands and giving it to Keith.

"Do you have anything by Arista Vineyards," he asked as he began to scan it over.

"Yea sweetie look toward the bottom," she answered.

"Ah yea, a good Pinot Noir sounds nice, but this doesn't sell by the glass, am I right," he inquired, holding up the list and pointing to a specific item.

"Let me see darling," Michelle said, pulling her glasses up on her nose and

following the direction of Keith's finger, "No sweetie that brand is only sold by the bottle," *she added.*

"Humm... and that's the only thing I see on here that compliments both our meals," *he said remorsefully.*

"I'm no sommelier but I do believe your right," *she replied.*

"Well... it's not my choice to make... Uh what..."

"No, no if you think it's right let's go with it," *I said interrupting them.*

"But it's nine..."

"The price doesn't matter to me, just bring it," *I said sternly, ending the debate before it started and staring Keith straight in the eye.*

"Ok I'll be right back with that, and if you still want to order dessert I'll take those orders when I get back with your bottle," *Michelle said, picking up the wine list, putting it back in her pouch, and walking away.*

"*Dude you know how much that wine cost!*" *Keith exclaimed.*

"*No and honestly I don't care, I ain't no broke nigga son and I didn't know you knew about wines. Not to mention how you just took charge and did what needed to be done, I'm impressed and that was kind of sexy bruh,*" *I replied.*

"*I might have come from the hood but I ain't get to be a junior partner at my firm by being a thug. I got some class and you seemed to be struggling with picking a wine so I just lent you a hand,*" *he said.*

"*Ok... you know while DaJuan and I were together a lot of money was spent on gifts and in the last six or seven months I guess you could say a spending account was setup for him. He also had a credit card and some access to mine, but what he didn't know was the bank account I allowed all that play in is just one of my accounts. I've been saving money since I was waiting tables and doing little side jobs in high school. Even though I was a big hoe in college, I was there on full academic scholarship so all the money that I made working my lil part time gig went to my savings account and it was the same in grad school. Now I make six figures a year, my ride is paid for, house is paid off, bills paid in advance, man I'm good... check this out though, the leach is out of my pocket now so those credit cards are about to get paid out and shut down and the cash I was spending stays in my pocket. I'm a keep that phone on till the contract end and maybe just use it now and then. See I was about to give dude the life and he fucked it up, but in reality that shit ain't hurt my pocket at all. I'm a businessman yo so I'll be writing some shit off come tax season my nigga," I announced proudly.*

"I feel you, but you kind of went left on me bruh, but..." Keith replied, hesitantly starting to say something else.

"Nah, nah I'm just saying I got money so spending a lil change on me and my homie ain't nothing, and... oh I see... I guess this shit stings more than I thought," I said, realizing what I'd just said and how it sounded.

"It's cool man, how bout we have a few glasses of wine and then I drive you home," he suggested.

"Only if you chill with me for a minute," I countered.

"Uh..."

"Don't worry I ain't gon try nothing, I'm just enjoying your company and don't want it to end yet," I interrupted.

"I ain't worried about you trying anything bruh," Keith laughed, "I just didn't expect that reply.

"Well, this evening was planned to end at my house anyway, preferably in my bedroom," I stated, glancing over in Clarissa and Jules' direction.

"So you wasn't gon bring me home when we finished," he asked.

"Hell nah, I paid yo way here you on your own getting back," I joked.

"That's fucked up son," Keith replied.

"Nah I'm playing man, I would have took you home or got you a cab, but since you agreed to chill with me I don't have to, at least not right away," I said.

"Yea ok, clean it up," he laughed.

"Here's your wine my loves did you still want to order dessert," Michelle inquired as she sat the bottle and a pair of glasses on the table.

"Uh yea, but I think we're gonna take them to go," Keith answered.

"Ok, well let me know when you're ready and I'll put those orders in for you," she said, turning to walk away.

"No we're ready now, but you don't have to fire the orders till I ask for the check," I said, gently catching her arm.

"Oh I'm sorry honey, I can absolutely do that, what can I get you guys," she stated apologetically.

"We'll take two molten chocolate cakes," Keith replied.

"Ok, I got it, just let me know when you all are ready so I can get it all together for you," she said, laying her hand on my shoulder again.

"You know Michelle if you just want to touch my muscles it's ok," I said, looking up at her.

"Honey you are too much," she laughed, walking away.

"So you hitting on the waitress now," Keith laughed.

"She kept touching me so I just asked if she wanted a lil feel," I replied.

Thirty minutes later Keith and I had just about finished the bottle of wine and both of us had a lil buzz from drinking so fast. I looked over to my left to see Clarissa sitting at her table alone, looking a little frustrated. The restaurant had gotten pretty full by this point and I figured her and her friend had decided not to pursue the bet any further.

"You think he dipped and left her with the bill," Keith asked, pulling me back to reality.

"Huh... oh... damn I hope not, but I don't think so," I replied.

"Hey guys, I saw that you were getting ready to wrap up your visit with us and I just wanted to make sure everything was ok," Linda chirped as she approached the table.

"Yes everything was great," I answered.

"Yea we started off a lil rough, but everything else from that point on was awesome love," Keith added.

"Well I'm glad it all worked out, please come back and visit us again guys," she stated cheerfully, *"Remember the next time the appetizers are on the house,"* she added before turning to leave.

"Well do we get a coupon or something, I mean if you and Michelle aren't here how will they know not to charge us for them and what if we don't come together," Keith asked.

"We don't really do coupons here, but Michelle will bring you both something when she brings your bill out," Linda stated.

"Ok great," he said.

"You can send Michelle on over with the bill and our desserts now," I chimed in.

"Sure thing, I'll send her right over! You guys have a great night," she exclaimed.

"Nigga! A coupon? This ain't no muthafuckin McDonald's son," I laughed.

"I'm just saying we needed something so the people would know not to charge us. Shit they even if they are here they might forget and it'll just be our word against theirs when the bill comes," he explained.

"Yea ok, I feel you, just the terminology was a little low class," I laughed.

"Aight whatever man," he stated, shaking his head and rolling his eyes.

"So my loves, I have your bill and I'll be back with your cakes in a few minutes," Michelle said as she sat the bill on the table.

"Awesome thanks a lot Michelle," I said, slipping my credit card into the jacket and handing it back to her.

"Thank you my love, and I'll be back for my feel, so unbutton that shirt baby boy," she laughed as she walked off.

"See you opened yourself up for that one," Keith joked.

"Yea you right, I did, but I'm sure she was joking," I replied.

"We'll see when she comes back," he laughed.

"Yea we will, but look oh girl still sitting over there by herself, maybe dude really did dip," I stated, directing my attention back over to Clarissa.

"Or maybe he's just in the bathroom taking a shit or something," Keith laughed, *"But I mean if you really worried about her*

maybe you should go over there and talk to her," he added.

"Nah I'm good bruh, I was just making an observation," I said coldly.

"Ok my loves, here are your desserts, here's your card, and here's a pen for you to sign the receipt. Now while you sign I'll touch," Michelle announced, narrating as she put everything down and placed a hand on my shoulder.

"Oh you were serious huh," I asked in surprise.

"You offered didn't you," she countered.

"Yea I did," I admitted.

"Ok then open that shirt up and let me claim what you offered," she exclaimed.

"Yea Paul, gon head and let the lady get what you offered her," Keith egged on.

"Shut up nigga," I snapped, opening the top two buttons on my shirt.

"Don't snap at him, you wrote this check hun," Michelle laughed before sliding her hand into my shirt.

"Oh shit... your hand is cold!" I shrieked.

"Sorry love, I'll try to make this quick," she apologized.

"I didn't say it was a bad thing, but it did catch me off guard," I laughed.

"Oh I can tell sweetie, but let me stop trying to get my groove back and let you guys get out of here," Michelle joked as she pulled her hand back.

"It's all good ma, everybody needs a little love now and then," I stated, slowly rising from my seat.

"Is that right," she laughed, placing a hand on her hip and looking over her glasses.

"Of course," I answered, embracing her tightly.

"Yea nobody deserves to be groove-less," Keith interjected, pulling her into his arms as soon as I released her.

"Is that even a word," I laughed.

"I don't think so baby, and yall young men better stop before I be catching a charge up in here," she stated bashfully, backing away from Keith and I, trying to hide her blushing face from us.

"Aww, you can't rape a willing victim," I joked.

"Humm, for a gay man, as you've been proclaiming all night, you sure have a way with women sir," she said.

"Well let's just say I get a lil itch for something different now and then," I laughed.

"Ok well I'll keep my mouth closed on that, but yall boys enjoy your night and hopefully I'll see yall around," Michelle replied, picking up the signed check from the table.

"I just might come back again when the moon is blue, I can't speak for him though," I said pointing to Keith.

"I'll definitely be back, and I hope to have you as my waitress again," Keith stated.

"Now there you go baby, speak up for yourself and don't let Mr. Man corrupt you too much now," she laughed.

"Oh you know it and I won't, but I think I'm bout as corrupt as I can get," he answered, flexing his pecs.

"Boy yall get out of here," she cried, playfully swinging her hand in our direction.

"Ok, ok have a good night Ms. Michelle," I replied as we turned to leave.

"Goodnight my loves," she called behind us.

"Looks like Clarissa isn't alone anymore," Keith said, pointing my attention back over to our "friend" from the office.

"I see, but there's still no sign of her gambling buddy," I answered making note that Jules was still MIA.

"I told you he probably dipped," he stated as we exited the restaurant.

"Well I hope not that would be real fucked up," I laughed, "But hey there was a Michael Kors watch I saw at the gift shop last time I was here, and I want to check it out if it's still here," I added.

"The gift shop is probably closed by now bruh," Keith declared, "and you can cover all that cleavage up now nigga," he continued, aiming at the buttons on my shirt.

"Cleavage! Nigga you trying say I got breast or something," I retorted.

"Maybe that was the wrong words to use, but yo shit is big bruh," he laughed.

"Whatever son, you just wanted to feel my on chest like Michelle did," I said.

"Nah bruh if I wanted to feel you up it wouldn't be just your chest son," he replied, playfully grabbing at my ass.

"Aye bruh don't let being tipsy get you in trouble," I warned, jerking away.

"Don't try to act like you don't like nobody smacking those cakes nigga," Keith replied, planting a solid lick on my ass.

"Shit... only when I'm deep in them guts my nigga, only when I'm in them guts," I stated, returning the blow.

"That shit only turns me on nigga," he laughed right before tripping over his own foot.

"Yea me too, but remind me not to give you no alcohol next time we go out," I laughed, catching him around the waist.

"I ain't drunk, the damn carpet was lumpy right there, and if you hadn't hit me on my ass so hard I would've been paying more attention to it," he countered, still stumbling and grasping on to me for balance.

"Oh I know you not drunk but you tipsy as hell nigga, but you need to pull it together before somebody sees us, well more importantly you, because I work for myself," I warned.

"Yea aight, I'm good, you can let me go... Wait a minute what's that supposed to mean yo," Keith stated aggressively, finally catching his center again and standing on his own.

"Nothing but you have a rep that you're building and need to protect my nigga that's all, but to think you said you were gonna drive me home, I'm glad I didn't take you up on that," I laughed.

"Again nigga I tell you I ain't drunk, and this gift shop is closed just like I thought it would be," he snapped, seeming a little annoyed.

"Hey man don't be mad at me for looking out for you, shit I could let you look crazy and go about my business son. However, I ain't that type of nigga," I retorted and headed back towards the restaurant.

"Aight, aight it just seem like you was throwing a brother under the bus for a sec, but ok I got you..."

"Hey aren't y'all the guys my girl was talking to in the restaurant," a man's voice interrupted from behind us.

"Ummm who's yo... oh yea we were," I stated somewhat hesitantly before realizing that it was Jules.

"Yea your Clarissa's friend right," Keith chimed in.

"Her husband actually, but yea we play that role sometimes because people can't always deal with my cuckold antics. You guys aren't backing out of the deal though are you?" he asked, smiling sort of eerily as he looked us over.

"So you ummm... do this type of thing..."

"Quite regularly, well as often as my wife wants too," Jules interjected cutting me off.

"I see but I guess there's two things you should know about me," I replied.

"Oh really? What would that be," he asked oblivious to the true weight of the bomb I was about to drop on him.

"For one he's gay," Keith chimed in.

"Really?" Jules shrieked almost excited by the announcement, but still exuding a good bit of disbelief.

"Yes really," I added, staring Keith down.

"What? You were gonna say it anyway weren't you," he replied.

"So I guess this means I can get in on the fun too huh," Jules asked with a big grin on his face.

"You don't have enough money to take this ride," I said smugly, noticing him tugging at his dick through his pants.

"No worries Mr. Mandingo I wouldn't try anything with those cakes, even though they

do look delightful," he assured me, "I like to suck dick and sometimes get my ass breed by a sexy bull," Jules added.

"These cakes feel good too," Keith interjected, grabbing a handful of my ass.

"Watch yourself nigga, and I'll pass sir," I answered, glaring at Keith and swatting his hand away, "Even though I'm a lil tipsy I'm not crazy and I'd never be interested in somebody like you drunk, tipsy, or otherwise," I continued, taking a step towards him.

"Paul let's just go bro," Keith interrupted, nervously grabbing my arm.

"Nah let me go bruh I'm good, I just want to let this weirdo know what I think about this bullshit game he trying to play with us," I said, yanking my arm away from him, "See that was kind of funny when you sent your bitch over to our table with that shady ass act, but you standing here trying to hit on me and my homie is pure bullshit. You think because you throw a little change around a muthafucka just gon roll with whatever you suggest. I ain't hurting for no money and neither is he but even if we were

you got some nerve approaching us like you did and you lucky I ain't knock yo weak ass out. Yea I'm gay so I'm not offended that you tried it, but the way you came at us is what pissed me off..."

"Paul I really think we should go now," Keith urged, wrapping his arm around my torso just as I took another step towards Jules.

"You don't think this bitch ass muthafucka needs a lesson in social etiquette," I yelped, turning to face Keith.

"Lesson in social etiquette? What the hell," he laughed, "Come on man let's get out of here before you really cause a scene," he insisted, noticing a few people stopping and starring.

"Hey man I didn't mean any harm, my wife and I liked what we saw and we just wanted to have a little fun. I offered you money because that's what most people want..."

"Save it dude and in the future be a little more careful who you approach and how you do it," Keith retorted, cutting him off, "Oh and

*we already had some fun with your lil wife,
better luck next time yo," he added before
dragging me back towards the door.*

Chapter 8

Just Crash Here

About ten or fifteen minutes later we were in my car headed to Keith's place. I wasn't sure why I snapped on Jules like that, but I'm glad that Keith was there to keep me from doing something that I might have regretted later. He had some nerve coming on to me like that though, especially that night after all that had happened and I'll admit I was a little buzzed. Keith and Brian aka "Black Hercules" fucking my lover in my house, in my house DaJuan was fucking over me like a chump. As the image began to playback in my head I caught myself glaring at Keith in disgust. Even though I somewhat believed his claim of not knowing that DaJuan was my dude a part of me didn't buy it at all. How could he not recognize my number or see my picture pop up on DaJuan's phone when I called? Better yet the nigga was in my house so how could he not see my awards, degrees, pictures, and name posted all over the place? I was starting to feel like he was trying to take advantage of me too. Talking all that bullshit about spending time with me and getting to know me better while we were at dinner, and my gullible ass was falling for it. All the anger and animosity I felt earlier came rushing back to me like a tsunami slamming into the coast of Hawaii. I think at that moment if looks could kill I would have been arrested for murder that night.

"Dude I'm sorry," Keith said, trying his best not to look me in the face, "I lied to you and I betrayed you, and I just can't live with keeping secrets from you. If you never want to speak to me again I completely understand, but if you can find it in your heart bruh please forgive me," he added reaching over to touch me sensing my fury.

"I don't know if I can just forgive you right at this moment but our friendship ain't gon end here. See every time you look at my face you gon have live with the fact that you were a part of the pain I'm in right now. I'm sure I'll get over it in time but right now the only thing you can do for me is give me some space or suck my dick," I replied, swiping his hand away.

"Huh," he grunted in confusion.

"You heard me nigga, either you give me some space tonight or you hang around and suck my dick," I reiterated.

"I don't get it, are you saying if I want to kick with you I got to suck yo dick?" he asked, looking like I was speaking a foreign language.

"That's an issue for you?" I inquired.

"Nah... I just don't really know how bruh... like real talk... before DaJuan came along I had never been with a dude and for the most part he's the only guy I've been fucking," he replied hesitantly.

"Oh really so you and Brain never had any one on one time?" I asked, ready to catch him in a lie.

"Nah, nah I thought about it but I never acted on it, we've only fucked together with DaJuan and even then there's minimal contact between us," he stated.

"Uh huh, so where did you meet Micah," I continued to interrogate.

"*We met at a party like he said,*" Keith answered.

"*A party huh, but you... humm... speak of the devil,*" I laughed, looking down at my phone to see a text from Micah as we pulled up to a stop light, "*He's texting me now,*" I added.

"*Micah?*" he asked.

"*Yeah and look what this nigga just sent me,*" I replied, passing him the phone as I pulled off.

"*Damn son... this shit is pretty... looks like a female's ass,*" he cried as he scrolled through the pictures of Micah bent over with his ass spread open and various other positions.

"*So you never saw that ass before nigga,*" I jeered.

"*Yeah I did earlier when you was about to fuck him,*" he answered, unmoved by my cynicism.

"Uh huh, that looks like yo dick in that picture right there, but back to this party, what kind of party was it," I questioned.

"It's not and it was a one of those lil freak parties like he was talking about tonight, and before you say anything this was only about maybe three months after DaJuan and I had went all the way for the first time. I wasn't even completely comfortable with the whole idea of going but he convinced me to try it out. So I went, but once niggas started showing up I bounced," he explained.

"So you just happened to be there long enough to run into Micah," I replied in disbelief.

"Nah Micah was already at the hotel when DaJuan and I got there. You must have missed the fact that these kats throw the parties together," Keith said, "It's a business partnership that was probably funded with your money," he continued.

"So you went to a sex party and didn't have sex with anybody," I asked.

"Paul are you hearing me? I'm telling you this dude... you know what never mind... and I didn't say I didn't have sex, I said I left when more people started showing up," he said, passing my phone back.

"I guess man, so you gon suck my dick or what," I said as well pulled up to another light.

"I don't mind doing it, but you'd have to teach me how. I know you don't believe me, but I'm not real experienced with all this bruh," he replied, "You should make a left at the next light," he added.

"Isn't your house in the Blairwood subdivision?" I asked.

"Yeah, but if you take this next left you can go around the back way and avoid some of these lights," he answered.

Ten minutes later we were driving up to Keith's driveway and I wasn't surprised to see the large but cozy looking bungalow seated at the heart of a quaint cul-de-sac. Next to his neighbors, his house seemed like a mini *mansion, however, I was still a little shocked to see how big the lots were in this neighborhood. As I pulled into the garage I noticed the blue F-150 that I'd grown accustomed to seeing him in with the extended cab, silver trim around the doors and dark tinted windows, and rims so shiny you could damn near see your reflection. I also saw the black and blue Suzuki sport bike that I rescued him from during a random thunderstorm one day after meeting him in the gym. That day was first of many rides I would give him and the beginning of our relationship. It was also during one of those rescue missions that I told him I was gay and he swore to me that he was 100% straight. I began to laugh to myself as I thought about the irony of that statement based on today's discoveries.*

"Paul are you coming in or you gonna sit out here and laugh all night bruh," Keith inquired as he got out, "What's so funny anyway," he added.

"Nothing bruh," I laughed.

"Come on now you act like I don't know you, tell me what's up for real," he urged.

"Nothing man I was just thinking about how a few years ago you swore up and down that you were straight. Now you getting ready to go in this house and suck my dick," I laughed, pulling my key from the ignition and sliding out of my truck.

"Whatever I still love and get plenty pussy my nigga," he stated.

"I never said you didn't bruh," I snickered as we entered Keith's den.

"But you still laughing though, and from the sound of it and that look in your eyes I know you got something on your mind Paul," he responded.

"So I can't laugh," I shrieked, dropping down in the first spot I got to like a ton of bricks.

"I mean I know I can't tell you what to do but I think I've known you long enough to know when something is up with you," Keith replied, disappearing behind the mini bar, "I'm bout to fix myself a lil drink you want something? How

*about a bottle of fruit juice or water?" he
added.*

*"Water is cool, but I think you already
know what's on my mind but I'm really trying
not to think about that too much right now. So
other than the fact that life has a way of
surprising you or changing the game up just
when you thought you had it on lock I'm good,"
I said.*

*"What does that mean?" he asked,
handing me two little bottles of ocean spray
juice as he took a seat in the corner of the chase
sectional where I was laying.*

*"I'm just saying I thought my life was
perfect and today I found out I've been a fool
all this time. I had my suspicions here and there
but I thought my relationship was going well.
Thought I was doing everything right and then I
come home to find you and Brian fucking my
dude," I said with regret, pausing a moment as
I sat up to check my phone, "I came home and
found the straightest nigga I know fucking my
dude," I added, giggling to myself.*

"Paul if I had known that you and dude was getting down like that I would have put you on game as soon as I found out. You were doing right, shit you were doing too right for a slimy muthafucka like him bruh," Keith said.

"Keith nigga I ain't got no issue with you man, so you ain't got to try to kiss my ass but you can lick it though," I laughed.

"I don't know about all that but how about you crash here tonight? We're both pretty tipsy and I wouldn't want you getting stopped by the cops or having an accident," he replied, dismissing my comments.

"Man nigga I ain't trying to lay on nobody's sofa I need a fucking bed to stretch out in son," I snapped.

"You see all this house I got bruh? I never said you had to sleep on the sofa, shit you could go in my room, shower, and take my bed if you want son," Keith answered.

"So what I'm a wear? I ain't got no clothes, I can't hang around this bitch naked," I stated.

"Why not nigga, I've seen you naked before," he laughed, *"Plus ain't nobody here but me and the housekeeper won't be here till bout ten or eleven,"* he added.

"How I know you won't try to take advantage of me while I'm sleep? Like you said we never really had any time together outside of the gym so we don't REALLY know each other," I said, continuing to give him a hard time.

"Shit maybe I shouldn't be offering yo ass nothing then if that's the case, but for real man quit making excuses. I know you probably got some shorts and whatnot out there in your gym bag. However, if you don't want to hang here or be around me it's cool I was just trying to look out for you bruh," Keith stated, taking a sip from his cup.

"Don't be so sensitive nigga," I cried, reaching up and smacking his thigh, *"After five years we should know a little something about each other. Besides I ain't leaving this muthafucka till you suck my dick,"* I continued, still rubbing his thigh.

"Whatever nigga quit rubbing on me like that with yo drunk ass," Keith groaned, pushing my hand away.

"So I can't touch you bruh? Aye you remember that time I gave you a massage in the sauna," I asked, still not moving my hand from his thigh.

"Which time?" he reiterated, curiously staring down at me.

"Shit there was more than one time huh," I laughed.

"Yea nigga there was but what about it son," he asked, getting impatient.

"I got a lil confession I need to make bout that bruh," I stated.

"I'm listening," he said urging me on.

"Don't rush me man I'm getting there," I said turning on my side to face him and inching closer, "but ummm... wait a minute I got to piss," I announced before hopping up from my spot and making a mad dash for what I thought was a bathroom.

"Really bruh? You gon sit there all that time, get me ready to hear a confession, and now you got to piss! Man you something bruh, and the bathroom is the next door down the hall. It should be open," he retorted.

"Damn why you put the bathroom so far down," I whined, grasping my dick as I ran down to the next door which was open as he said. Thankfully it was because I might have pissed on myself if I had waited any longer.

Chapter 9

Ok I'll Confess

About ten minutes later I returned to the den boasting about how good it felt to drain the pipe. Keith just sat there sipping from his cup and staring at me. The look on his face let me know that he hadn't forgotten about the grand confession I was supposed to be making. However, I'd kind of lost my nerve by that point, but I knew he wouldn't let up till I said something so there was no backing out. I thought about just making up something, but I figured he knew me well enough to know when I was bullshiting. So I just sat down and began to tell him about how turned on I'd get while I was giving him those massages in the sauna.

I'm not even sure what made him ask me to rub his shoulders that day but I didn't mind. Over the last couple days before that Keith had been complaining about how it was bothering him so I agreed to help him out. I also advised him to go get it checked out just in case something was wrong with it. He gave me some lame excuse about not having time so I just left it alone and proceeded with the *massage. After all I had not long ago added a massage therapy certification to my list of credentials so it was a perfect opportunity to get in some practice. Not to mention Keith was sexy as hell and I kind of always had a secret desire to feel his muscles. Even though he wasn't as big as me standing at 5'9 and weighing roughly between 175 and 180lbs. He was incredibly toned and had a nicely proportioned physique. Let's not forget to mention the pair of gorgeously rounded, caramel cakes that I'd caught myself staring at from time to time. Anyway, I'm getting a little ahead of myself. So I told him about how my dick throbbed and how I wanted to slide my tongue between his cheeks. Yet I dared not test the waters because I knew he was straight and I didn't want to disrespect him.*

For the next couple minutes after I finished my "confession" there was an awkward silence in the room as Keith just sat there drinking his drink. I wondered if I had made a mistake telling him and contemplated leaving, but I wasn't really sure of that either.

I guess he was processing everything as he continued to slowly sip on his drink and stare blankly at me as if he was waiting for more. Then just as I aimed to get up he quickly put his cup down, grabbed me by the arm, and pulled me close. Within seconds our lips were locked in one of the most passionate kisses I'd ever had. I was shocked and didn't know what to do or say and I couldn't bring myself to pull away from him. Lost and vulnerable in my own thoughts I tried to find some logic in what was happening. Then after what seemed like an hour he released me.

"I've been wanting to do that all night," he said, grabbing his cup and laying back on the sofa again, "and if you wanted to eat my ass so bad you should've just did it if that's what you wanted. I mean how many straight dudes just randomly sit in the sauna and get massages," he added.

Once again I was stunned by how naive I had been. Keith had basically given me a couple opportunities and I had missed them all. Was I really that blind or did I just block

114

out the possibility because I just knew that he was straight. Then again I was in what I thought was a committed relationship so even though my hormones may have been saying do it I'd never act on those feelings. Now that I think about it though, it was about four months ago when he first asked me to give him a massage and the timing lines up with the time that he said he started messing around with DaJuan. Damn I must be losing my touch for real because any other time I could sniff that stuff out from a mile away.

"What you got in that cup bruh," I asked, thinking maybe he was just talking crazy since we were both a little tipsy.

"Grey Goose Magnum and cranberry juice but I ain't drunk, maybe a lil tipsy, but I ain't drunk," he replied as he got up and made his way back to the bar.

"Nigga you drinking vodka and got me over here with fruit juice," I scolded.

"That's right because your ass is already drunk. Anytime you get ready to fight

*somebody in Harrah's casino over a petty
proposition that you could have just said no to
and walked away from there's an issue. Shit I
understand you being offended but I don't
think it was worth a fight. Especially not with
some fuckin white dude, that's why I pulled
your ass on out of there," Keith laughed,
"Plus I had a feeling that ole boy would have
gotten a lot more than he'd bargained for if
you got the chance to lay your hands on him,"
he continued.*

"What you mean by that?" I asked.

*"My grandmother used to always tell
my mom and aunts to never whip us while
they were mad because they just might kill us.
I think that with all you been through today
your fuse was already cut short and you had
been drinking. Probably had a lil taste before
we met up," he replied.*

*"I might have had a lil sip but I wasn't
tipsy till we started drinking that wine you
suggested," I answered.*

"Yea well, there you have the reason why I have what I have in my cup and you are on juice duty," he laughed.

"Whatever bruh, give me some," I commanded, making my way over to the bar.

"Give you some what my dude? Some of these cakes? Some dick? What you want bruh," he taunted, "and since we're confessing tonight I only asked you give me those massages because I thought it might just lead to something else. I was a little nervous about asking the first time but it got a little easier the last three. Since you always be talking shit about my ass I thought you would have at least tried to grab it while I was vulnerable to you," he stated, making it obvious that I was truly blinded by something.

"Yea well... I thought you were straight and regardless of whether or not I was attracted to you I'd never disrespect you, plus I was with DaJuan," I responded.

"True but unfortunately..."

"Don't remind me, I already know. Now about you wanting to kiss me all night, where that shit come from," I inquired, taking a seat on one of the bar stools.

"Just like in the sauna bruh, maybe I just wanted to try something new. Over the past couple months a lot has changed in my world and I'm not completely sure how I feel about it but you only live once right?" he said, finally handing me a cup of vodka and cranberry juice.

"That's true but..."

"Hold on let me finish," he interjected.

"Ok go head," I conceded.

"About a month ago I read this story about how this dude and another had basically been friends forever and throughout all the years they'd known each other neither of them knew that the other got down. They was like best friends but that was the one thing they never shared with each other. Then one night they both went to this freak party

*and caught each other red handed fucking
and getting fucked by other dudes. One friend
was supposed to be going out with his girl
and the other was supposed to be chilling at
the crib watching movies and shit, but low
and behold here they both end up at the party.
Now after that night things were a little
awkward between for like a day or so till one
of the dudes reached out to the other and was
like we need to talk bruh. Come on let's go
back over here, I need to sit down with this
shit," he said, motioning for me to follow him
back to the sofa.*

*"You can't handle that shit huh," I
joked as I sat down next to him.*

*"This my third drink bruh," he
informed me.*

*"No wonder that shit going to your
head you drinking that shit too fast, but finish
telling me about these dudes you read about,"
I replied.*

*"Oh yea, so one of them finally reached
out and said we need to talk. So they met that*

night at local bar, order food and drinks, and began the difficult conversation about why they'd kept this secret from each other. They both had their reasons but they were supposed to be best friends so it hurt a little to find out the way they did," he said.

"I can imagine that being both shocking and embarrassing to both, so what happened next," I stated, urging him to continue on.

"Well they hatched out their differences and promised to never keep anymore secrets but as I read on there was another secret that came out and changed everything between them," he continued.

"What was that," I asked anxiously.

"The one with the girl had been secretly in love with the other," Keith said.

"What? Man that really does sound like some old storybook type shit, so did they end up getting together in the end?" I questioned sarcastically.

"Well they did get together but that wasn't the end," he replied.

"Ok so what happened next then, I can't imagine it not stopping with a classic storybook ending," I said.

"That would have been nice but he cheated on me repeatedly. Every time he said baby I'm sorry or it won't happen again I believed him like a fool. I left my girl, moved out of my apartment, fucked up my credit, all to be with a man that fucked over me like a complete stranger," he explained.

"Damn that's fucked up... wait a minute did you just say you? I..."

"I already know what you're about to say and I made up that lame story I told you earlier bout DaJuan hitting on me at the gym. Truth is I've been messing with dudes on and off since my freshman year of college. I actually met DaJuan at one of him and Micah's exclusive parties after being invited by Micah over a party line," he chimed in before I could try and piece it together.

"Hold on, hold on you mean to tell me that you lied to me again dude? Is that really what you're saying? Now all of this is supposed to be the truth? I'm not too sure I want to hear anymore bruh," I snapped, jumping up and heading towards the door.

"Paul wait! I wanted to tell you earlier I wanted to tell you a long time ago but I never really had the nerve to before now," Keith cried, "Please come sit back down so we can talk about this," he pleaded.

For about a minute I just stared at him, standing there blocking the door as if I couldn't just throw him to the side. I struggled with the decision of doing just that or staying and hearing him out. Something in that moment did seem sincere and I wanted to believe him but all he'd given so far was lies. What was I supposed to think after everything that happened today? At that moment it seemed like the only people I could really trust was God and myself.

Chapter 10

New Start

"I know you're stronger than me and all but I'm not gonna let you leave. Besides I hid your keys while you were in the bathroom," Keith said.

"So tell me why I shouldn't just toss yo ass around and make you give up my keys," I growled threateningly.

"Because I've been in your shoes before bruh, confused, hurt, angry, and disappointed not so much in a dude but in yourself for not seeing what was going on. Paul believe me bro, no more lies no more secrets let's just talk," he tried to reason.

"Aight, I don't know why I'm agreeing to this but ok," I replied.

"When I told you there was something familiar about the look in your eyes it was because it was the same look I had after having my heart trampled by Brian," Keith stated.

"Brian? Black Hercules Brian?" I reiterated, slowly sitting back down.

"Yea, we didn't work out as lovers but we were able to reconcile our feelings and salvage our friendship. Not to mention the drama was almost three years ago and I couldn't allow myself to live with resentment in my heart," he said, taking a seat beside me.

"I get the forgiveness bit but I don't know if I'd want him in my personal space like you guys were earlier today," I replied.

"Yea I know call me crazy but somehow I'm cool with it. Brian and I have been friends since we were kids and nearly every important event in our lives was shared with the other," Keith responded as he finished up his drink.

"I don't know bruh, sounds like you still have some deep feelings for this dude that you're trying to mask as just being a devoted friend, or is there something else you haven't told me yet" I said, staring him down curiously.

"Well I don't know how you'd feel about it but about a year and a half ago Brian

was rushed to the emergency room after a sudden onset of sharp pains hit him at work. I was listed as one of his emergency contacts so they called me after they couldn't get in touch with the other two. When I got there the doctor said it appeared to be a sickle cell crisis but they would have to do some test to properly diagnose him. I was scared to death when they called me and now knowing there's a possibly that he might have some life-threatening disease made me even more nervous. I asked if I could see him and they told me I'd have to wait till all the test were done," he stated, recalling what seemed to be a painful moment.

"Well he obviously got better from whatever it was right," I asked.

"Yea it turned out to just be iron deficiency, but with all that happened our friendship was revived. I guess it's true that crisis can actually bring people together because we hadn't talked in almost a year before that happened," Keith answered.

"I guess I can understand the notion of a friendship being stronger than any drama or feelings of resentment especially when one of you is going through something even more traumatic. Tell me this though bruh, in five years how the fuck did I not clock yo ass," I laughed, trying to change subjects.

"Honestly I'm not sure, but I mean we only really saw each other at the gym and if you had never told me about your situations I probably would have never known either," he replied.

"Maybe so, but it's all out in the open now right? No more lies or secrets," I said.

"They always say that alcohol bares the soul, but in my case I guess it just encouraged me to do and say some things I've been wanting to for years. When you told me you were gay it wouldn't have been the best opportunity to share because I was with Gina and struggling with my feelings for Brian and I just didn't want to complicate anything for anybody," Keith said, "Now if you can *forgive me for bending the truth and keeping my secrets maybe we can call this a new start," he added.*

"Yea I can dig that I guess, but if I catch your ass in a lie we fighting nigga," I threatened while giving a halfhearted smile.

"Copy that bruh, but I don't have any reason to hold anything back from you now," he replied, taking note that I was serious even though I played it as a joke.

"Ok well you still haven't sucked my dick yet," I stated nonchalantly.

"Is that really the way you want to start off our new chapter," Keith laughed.

"Nigga don't play innocent, you knew when we walked in the door you was supposed to suck my dick. I told you in the car you had two options, either give me some space or suck my dick. Then you said you didn't mind doing it but you wasn't all that good at it. I don't really believe that now since

I know you're not the novice to messing around that I thought you were," I said.

"Ha ok I'll take that, but since I changed the game up how about this," he replied, putting his hand on my shoulder and waiting for a signal to proceed.

"What?"

"If I suck your dick, you got to eat my ass, but let's shower first and then we can take it to the bed," he suggested.

"Well after what I told you earlier you should already know I don't have a problem with eating your ass," I laughed.

"Ok bet then," Keith replied, rising from the sofa and extending his hand for me to follow him.

After that not many more words were spoken that night. Keith led me down the hall and up the stairs to the master bedroom. When we got there he took me by the hand, led me through the dark room, and sat me down on the bed. He then disappeared into the dimly lit bathroom and emerged again beckoning for me to come in and vanished again. After taking off my shoes, I slowly navigated through the darkness using the light from the bathroom as a guide. It was only maybe ten feet from the bed to the bathroom door but I still moved cautiously being unfamiliar with my surroundings. As I stepped into the bathroom I could smell the scent of lavender and vanilla. The shower was roaring and there were two sets of towels laid out on the counter. I proceeded to get undressed but Keith immediately pulled my hands away and told me that he wanted to pamper me a little and I could just relax. Curious about what he meant I stopped and just stood there until further instruction was given.

A few minutes later, after adjusting the water temperature a couple times, he turned his attention back to me. The look in his eyes was one I'd never seen in my life. Especially from him, during our workouts together there was always fire there, but not like this. They were full of passion yet warm and inviting as if he was allowing me to see into his soul. He pulled me close and slowly began unbuttoning my shirt, exposing my cleavage as he'd called it earlier that night. Initially there was a slight chill when the air hit my skin but Keith's warm hands quickly changed that. His deep brown eyes had me mesmerized and my body quivered with excitement. As he began to unbuckle my belt and open my pants my dick started to tingle in anticipation. I balanced myself sort of clumsily on Keith's shoulders as he helped me out of my pants and then my socks. With only one last item of clothing now standing between me and completely nudity he sat back and quietly looked me over before proceeding disrobe himself. Once totally naked he pulled me close again and started gently kissing my neck. A soft moan escaped my lips while the intensity of the moment grasped my mind. Keith's lips continued to meander down my body caressing my soul with each carefully placed kiss. When he got down to my waist he playfully tugged at my boxers with his teeth and slid his open mouth over my dick. The warmth of his breath seeping through the thin material instantly caused my dick to throb and demand freedom from the confines of my underwear.

About five minutes later the warm, soothing blanket of the shower enrobed our bodies. Keith took his time lathering me up, making sure not to leave a spot untouched. The combination of the water, Keith's hands, and the sweet aroma emanating from the candles was starting to push me overboard. It was a force of attraction that couldn't be resisted and my instincts were getting hard to tame. I didn't want to rush the moment but all this teasing was getting to me. I started to become weak in the knees and had to lay against the wall to keep from falling. Keith just continued lathering and rinsing and then without any warning he leaned over and started sucking my dick. I was caught off guard and the only thing I could do was hold on tight and enjoy the ride.

"Damn nigga, I thought you said you weren't good at this shit," I moaned,

*grabbing the back of his head to take some
control of the situation.*

*His only response was to keep sucking
until I was damn near ready to cum. Then
everything stopped abruptly. He stood upright
again, turned off the water, grabbed a towel
from the counter and stepped out of shower. I
just stood there with my back against the wall,
dick still standing at full attention and waiting
for an encore. Confused and a little agitated
from being robbed of the good nut I was
about to shoot down his throat I pulled myself
off the wall. I remember thinking how could
he just tease a nigga like that as I watched
him dry off and then wrap the towel around
his waist. It didn't make it any better that
while he was drying off he had his back to me
and you know those cakes were screaming at
me. He then grabbed the other towel from the
counter and turned to me with a deceivingly
innocent smile. I laughed to myself and
stepped out of the shower allowing him to dry
me off as well before we went back into the
bedroom.*

"You can go head on in the room, I'll be there in a few," he instructed before turning to get something out of the cabinet.

"Ok," I replied dryly, still a little salty because he didn't let me cum.

"Don't be mad bruh I'm a take care of you real good when I get in the room," he called behind me.

Like a spoiled child I just went in the room and didn't answer. As I laid there I couldn't help but think about how good his mouth felt and that soft ass that I finally got a chance to get my hands on. The vision of him bent over in front of me haunted my mind and I could feel my dick throbbing again. I fought back the urge to stroke it but with every second that passed by I was starting to lose the battle. Then finally Keith emerged from the bathroom wearing nothing but a smile and toting a tray with two candles, baby oil, and another bottle that looked like whipped cream. He placed the tray down on the nightstand and instructed me to lay on my stomach before climbing up on the bed with one of the candles. The first thing that came to mind was how I was going to lay flat on my stomach with a hard dick. No matter what I tried I knew it was gonna be a hassle and I was going to be uncomfortable till it went back down. My second thought was what in the hell was he planning to do with that candle? Thinking back a couple years I remembered how hot wax and I weren't the best of friends. There was a sigh of relief when I saw him put it down on the other side of the bed. He then warned me I might feel something cold as he reached for the bottle of baby oil and drizzled some on my back. It wasn't as bad as I thought it would be but it still sent a chill up my spine, but Keith's warm hands quickly relieved that.

After about fifteen minutes Keith asked me to turn over on my back. I obliged, being careful to keep the towel underneath me so the oil wouldn't get on his sheets. He then proceeded to massage my chest, arms, feet, and the front of my legs. Every so often his hand would brush against my nuts or he'd shift my dick from one side to the other as he worked his way around. I wasn't expecting this at all but I was surprised by how good he was at massages and I was the one with the license. The way he rubbed and squeezed and caressed my body made me completely forget about all the bullshit with DaJuan. He asked me to turn over again so he could catch the back of my legs. I found it strange that he didn't do them the first time but then again I'm the professional, he's not. So I turned over again and allowed him to continue. Even though his method of progression was a bit off his hands felt great. However I still wondered what else his had in mind as the other item on the tray caught my eye again. Keith advised me to brace myself for the cold oil again. As I prepared myself to feel the chill of oil I got another surprise. I almost jumped out of my skin when I felt Keith's tongue slither through the crack of my ass.

"You said I could lick it didn't you," he laughed, noticing my reaction.

"You got jokes now huh nigga," I replied, biting my bottom lip in effort to compose myself while he continued eating my ass.

"I'm just saying you offered earlier so I just saw the opportunity and took it," Keith continued to laugh, "but you can turn back over now," he added.

"I wasn't complaining it just caught me off guard bruh," I said as I turned over again.

"Yea ok... well it's time for you to hold up your end of the bargain," he stated.

"What you mean my end of the bargain?" I asked, watching him straddle my lap with his ass facing me.

"I suck your dick, you eat my ass," he reminded me.

"Oh ok, that explains why you stopped all of a sudden in the shower," I said, sliding my arms around his thighs as he got in position for me to dive in tongue first.

"Nah I just did... didn't want... damn yo... shit," he stammered as I spread his cheeks and slowly began to slide my tongue around his hole.

"You didn't what bruh," I teased, knowing that I had him where I wanted him.

"I didn't want you to cum yet nigga," he moaned.

For the next ten minutes I indulged myself in those caramel cakes of his. Out of all the crazy shit that had happened that day this was one thing I had no issue doing. Keith moaned and rocked his ass back on my tongue which instantly made my dick stand up. I closed my eyes and in my mind I could see myself pounding his ass mercilessly. So many times I had dreamed about getting this nigga in bed but I never thought it would really happen. I was shocked from my fantasy by the feeling of his mouth on my dick. At that point my hormones were in overdrive and I almost shot my load down his throat. His ass tasted so sweet and that mouth felt like heaven. I was

doing my best to keep control but the more he
sucked the harder it was to contain myself.
Then all of a sudden he flipped around and
centered my dick right at the entrance of his
hole. He grasped my chest tightly as the head
began to slide pass his golden gate. In awe,
all I could do was lay there while my dick was
being sucked into what had to be one of the
tightest asses I'd ever had. Then just as he got
it balls deep and started to grind on it reality
hit me. I was HIV positive and fucking this
man raw. I tried to stop him, reminding him of
my condition but he flipped the script on me
saying that he was positive too. What the fuck,
another secret, but I couldn't get upset in that
moment. I could only focus on how good that
ass was starting to feel. Still the little voice in
my head wouldn't let me rest because I knew I
shouldn't be fucking without a condom.
Finally I convinced Keith to stop and get one.
I knew I was risking killing the vibe but I just
couldn't allow him to take that chance.
However, once that condom was on I did just
what I had always dreamed of doing. We
fucked for what seemed like hours and when

we woke up the next morning it was on again. When I go on that plane the day before I had plans of spending a romantic evening with my dude and ending it in that luscious ass of his yet I walked into the shock of my life. Still that wasn't such a bad thing because I still got some ass and now I didn't have to worry about if my dude was faithful.

Chapter 11

My Buddy

So I've been officially single for three months and now you know why. Keith and I have been kicking it a good bit since that night and I'll go ahead and tell you that nigga got some good fucking ass. Just thought I'd add that in just in case somebody was wondering. Although we haven't made anything official, other than being friends with benefits I think this relationship could be something nice. He spoils me, I spoil him, and it's all just good, no strings attached fun. Now let me be clear, when I say spoil we treat each other to movies, lunch, dinner, and small gifts here or there, but it's only been three months so there haven't been many "gifts" given. I doubt I'll ever do what I did for DaJuan for anybody else unless we've signed some papers and even then they'll be some restrictions. Keith has his own money though so I'm not too worried about that.

Now since I brought DaJuan up I guess I'll give you an update on what happened after I put him out. If you recall I went ham and cut off the credit cards, put a freeze on the phone, and the next day I had all the locks on my doors changed, reported the phone stolen, and took his name off my gym membership. It's not like he was going to the gym to work out anyway and he definitely wasn't gonna continue living on my dime. However, I haven't seen or heard from him since that day, but I have heard about him. Supposedly he either quit or lost his job at Harrah's and has been crashing with Micah or whoever dick he's sucking that night. Keith even told me he thinks he saw him at Rawhide one night. I guess it's hard when you have a good thing and then get it snatched away because you want to be a hoe. Not sure I'll ever understand why some people choose to make life hard for themselves.

Now the party that Micah haphazardly mentioned that they were planning still when on, but things got a little out of hand and a couple people spent the night in jail. I don't have all the details on that, but it's rumored that some chick crashed it looking for her man after finding the text in his phone. I'm not one to gossip though so I'll leave the hearsay to the rumor mill. Well maybe I'll say one more thing. The part that's even crazier is the man the woman was looking for just happened to be Brian. Go figure right, and I bet you already know who he called to get him out of jail right? So maybe I do have a few more facts, but I won't be the one to throw shade.

I sometimes wonder what would have happened if I hadn't caught him in action that day. Even though I had suspicions there wasn't any solid evidence that he was cheating other than acting weird on the phone sometimes. Now since I cut him off I did a little investigating and found out that he had in fact been using my money to throw those parties. There was thousands of dollars spent on flyers, alcohol, hotel rooms, condoms, lube, and a bunch of other miscellaneous things. I'm actually surprised that I didn't catch this sooner, but I was too busy being entrepreneur of the year and loving being in love to see anything. These dudes were really doing it big though, and making a killing with it. If I thought I could get away with it I'd setup some sessions too, but I left that life alone for reason.

Well, anyway I have a flight to catch in about two hours and I promised Keith I'd stop by and see him before I leave. You know after spending all this time with him and getting to know him better I don't understand how Brian would let him slip away. Then again, I guess a lot of people could say the same about me. Still I won't rush into anything, after all I did walk in on this dude running a train my ex. Yet I'm still hopeful that one day I'll find something real, and if things keep going the way they are it just might be with him. Am I crazy? I guess so, but you only live once and everybody knows that love don't really love nobody.